Charles Dickens

A TALE OF TWO CITIES

Sweet Cherry

THE
Charles
Dickens
CHILDREN'S COLLECTION

Published by Sweet Cherry Publishing Limited
Unit 36, Vulcan House,
Vulcan Road,
Leicester, LE5 3EF
United Kingdom

First published in the UK in 2020
2020 edition

2 4 6 8 10 9 7 5 3

ISBN: 978-1-78226-487-3

© Sweet Cherry Publishing

Charles Dickens: A Tale of Two Cities

Based on the original story from Charles Dickens,
adapted by Philip Gooden.

Cover design by Pipi Sposito and Margot Reverdiau
Illustrations by Pipi Sposito

Lexile® code numerical measure L = Lexile® 630L

Guided Reading Level = Q

www.sweetcherrypublishing.com

Printed and bound in Turkey
T.IO006

PARIS

A very long time ago in Paris, a doctor called Alexandre Manette was released from prison. He had been locked up for eighteen years. He was in prison not because he had done something wrong, but because he had stood up for what was right.

In doing the right thing, Dr Manette made enemies. Powerful enemies who threw him into prison. In those days, the rich and powerful ruled France. Ordinary people were kept poor and hungry. But anger and despair were bubbling beneath the surface. In a few years there would be a violent revolution. It would bring about the deaths of the King and Queen of France, and many of the rich and powerful.

Our story starts a few years before the revolution, just after Dr Alexandre Manette was freed from prison. He had moved into a room above a tavern, in a poor area of Paris. The owners of the tavern, Monsieur and Madame Defarge, were friends of his.

Dr Manette's mind was scarred by his experience in prison. The one good thing that had happened there was that he had taught himself how to make shoes. Now he clung to his workbench and tools as if they were the only things in the whole world that he could trust.

One day, the door to his gloomy attic room opened. There stood Monsieur Defarge, a beautiful young woman and an older man.

'You have visitors,' said Monsieur Defarge.

Dr Manette did not look up from his workbench.

'Here is a gentleman who knows a well-made shoe when he sees one,' said Monsieur Defarge. 'Show him the shoe you are working on, Manette.'

The older man, whose name was Jarvis Lorry, took the shoe in his hand.

'Tell him what kind of shoe it is, and the maker's name,' said Defarge.

'It is a lady's shoe,' said Dr Manette softly, still not looking up.

'And the maker's name?'

'One Hundred and Five, North Tower,' said Dr Manette.

Mr Lorry realised Dr Manette was saying his old prison cell number instead of his name.

'One Hundred and Five, North Tower,' the Dr Manette repeated.

'Do you recognise me, Dr Manette?' said the young woman.

Dr Manette kept looking at his work.

The woman moved towards him. Although her face was young and Dr Manette's was old, anyone looking at them side by side would have thought that they looked alike.

The shoemaker caught sight of the hem of her dress as she neared him. He looked up and stared at her.

'Are you the jailer's daughter?' he asked vaguely.

The young woman's name was Lucie. Her golden hair tumbled down her neck. The shoemaker reached up, took a curl in his hand and peered at it. Lucie laid her hand on his shoulder.

Monsieur Defarge and Jarvis Lorry watched from the doorway. They hardly dared to breathe.

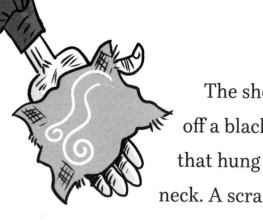

The shoemaker took off a blackened string that hung round his neck. A scrap of folded rag was attached to it. He opened the rag carefully, on his knee. Inside were two long threads of golden hair.

Dr Manette reached for the woman's golden curls again. His eyes moved from them to the strands in his hand.

'They're the same. How can it be?' he asked in wonder. 'She laid her head upon my shoulder that night when I was taken away. When I was brought to the North Tower, I found these few hairs upon my sleeve. I have kept them ever since to remind me …'

The shoemaker was too tearful to continue. Lucie wrapped her arms around him.

'We have come to take you away from here,' she said. Her voice was on the edge of tears, too. 'We are going to England, to London.'

Lucie was Dr Manette's daughter.
He had last seen her when she was
a little golden-haired child. Lucie's
mother, who was English, had died
soon after her husband's
imprisonment. Then
Lucie's guardian, Jarvis
Lorry, had taken her to
live in England. Lucie
had not seen her father
again until that very moment, in the
attic room in Paris.

Soon after, the three of them
– father, daughter and guardian –
boarded the carriage that would take

them out of Paris. They were waved off by Monsieur and Madame Defarge.

When the travellers reached Calais on the French coast, they got on a boat to Dover. Dr Manette was still weak and confused. There were only a handful of other passengers. One of them, a young and handsome Frenchman called Charles Darnay,

took pity on Dr Manette. Lucie was
very grateful to him. He was kind to
them and helped find them the most
sheltered spot on the small ship.

Lucie and her father were happy in London, and, day by day, he began to get better. Lucie sometimes thought of Charles Darnay, though she did not expect to see him again.

LONDON

The criminal court in London was known as the Old Bailey. It was full of people. They had come to watch the trial of a spy. Eager faces strained around pillars and corners for a glimpse of the person standing in the dock.

He was a young and handsome man, about twenty five years old. His name was Charles Darnay. It was the Frenchman who, four years ago, had been kind to Dr Manette and Lucie on the boat.

The trouble was that Charles Darnay was French. Britain and France were not at war, but the two countries were very suspicious of each other. And Darnay seemed to have been behaving oddly.

Against their will, Dr Manette and Lucie were called as witnesses against Charles Darnay. The lawyer, who was trying to prove Darnay was a French spy, asked his first question.

'Miss Manette, have you seen the prisoner before?'

'Yes, sir,' said Lucie.

'Where?'

'On board the boat that brought my father and me to England.'

'Did you talk with the prisoner on that journey across the Channel?'

'Yes, sir.'

'Tell us about it.'

Looking fondly at Charles Darnay standing in the dock, Lucie said: 'When the gentleman came on board the boat—'

'The gentleman?' said the lawyer. 'Do you mean the prisoner?'

'Yes, sir.'

'Then say "prisoner".'

'When the – the prisoner came on board, he noticed that my father was very weak. The prisoner was kind and gentle to us.'

'Never mind all that,' said the
lawyer. 'Did the prisoner tell you that
he was travelling under a false name?'

'He told me that he was travelling on secret business that might get people into trouble. That is why he did not use his real name.'

Seeing how bad her words made Darnay look, Lucie began to weep.

'Monsieur Darnay is a good man, I am sure,' she pleaded.

'Never mind all that,' replied the lawyer.

The last thing the lawyer wanted was for Lucie's words to convince the jury that Charles Darnay was innocent.

Then something odd happened.

Another witness was called. He said that he had seen Darnay hanging around near a dockyard. He believed that the Frenchman could have been spying on the soldiers and sailors who worked there.

The lawyer defending Darnay was called Mr Stryver. Sitting next to him was an untidy man, who lounged casually on the bench. This man nudged Mr Stryver and whispered in his ear.

Mr Stryver asked the witness: 'Are you quite sure it was the prisoner you saw near the dockyard?'

'Quite sure,' said the witness.

'Have you ever seen anybody who looks like the prisoner?'

'I don't think so,' said the witness.

'Look carefully at this gentleman here,' said Mr Stryver, pointing to the man lounging next to him. 'And now look carefully at the prisoner again.

They look very like each other, don't they?'

It was true, they did look very alike. Especially when the untidy man, whose name was Sydney Carton, took off his wig.

Everyone in the courtroom gasped and nodded in agreement. People started to talk among themselves:

'Those two men might almost be twins.'

'They're doubles!'

'That witness can't be trusted.'

'And the nice young lady thinks the prisoner is innocent.'

'Quiet!' the judge bellowed. The courtroom fell silent once more.

The jury went away to consider its verdict. Was Charles Darnay guilty or not guilty of spying for France?

After several anxious hours, the verdict came back: not guilty.

Afterwards, Charles Darnay thanked Sydney Carton, the man who looked so much like him.

'It was nothing,' said Carton carelessly. 'I don't know why I did it, anyway.'

Sydney Carton was altogether a careless young man. He was a friend of the lawyer, Mr Stryver, and sometimes helped him in his work. But he had never cared much about other people – or about himself. Now, however, Sydney Carton envied Charles Darnay for one thing. He had seen the way Lucie gazed fondly at the accused man in the dock. No one had ever looked at *him* in that way. Even so, he was glad that he had helped to save Darnay.

The love between Charles Darnay and Lucie grew quickly. The Frenchman earnt his living by teaching French to people in London. He often visited the house where Lucie lived with her father.

Dr Manette was pleased to see his daughter fall in love with the young Frenchman, whom he liked very much. In those days, men often asked fathers for permission to marry their daughters. When Darnay asked Dr Manette, he agreed at once.

On the morning of the wedding, Darnay wanted to speak to Dr Manette in private. When the two men finally came out of the doctor's room, Dr Manette's face had turned as white as his hair.

What had passed between the father and the man about to become his son-in-law? What words had been spoken?

No one knew, and the wedding went ahead as planned. As the couple left for their honeymoon, Dr Manette and his daughter embraced.

'Take care of her, Charles,' said the doctor.

More time passed. In London, Lucie and Charles Darnay lived happily with Dr Manette. The couple had a daughter. She had long golden hair like her mother's.

Sydney Carton was a frequent visitor to the house. He enjoyed their company and they enjoyed his. He was very fond of Lucie and of her little family.

But, while things were calm in London, there was a violent storm brewing in Paris.

PARIS

One day, outside Monsieur and
Madame Defarge's tavern, a cask of
wine tumbled off the back of
a cart. The cask cracked
apart when it hit the
ground. Red wine spilt
across the muddy
stones of the street.

At once, all the people nearby
stopped what they were doing and
ran to the spot. Some tried to scoop

up thin streams of wine in their cupped hands. Others tried to catch the precious red liquid in broken cups and bowls. Some even took pieces of wine-soaked wood from the shattered cask and chewed them. They were so thirsty, they would have licked the wine off the road itself!

They looked like scarecrows. Their hands and their mouths and their ragged clothes were all stained red. The stains were from the wine, but they were the colour of blood.

As if this were a signal, the poor people of Paris seemed to come together like one vast creature. A creature with thousands of arms and legs.

Steel blades and wooden sticks waved in the air. Voices filled the narrow, dirty streets with a sound like thunder.

The hands of Madame Defarge were no longer occupied with knitting needles. Now she grasped an axe. Her belt held a pistol and a sharp knife.

'Come, then!' cried Monsieur Defarge. 'Fellow citizens and friends, we are ready! To the Bastille!'

The Bastille was the prison where Dr Manette had been kept years before. It was not far from the Defarge's tavern. With its eight great towers and battlements, the Bastille looked like a castle.

The crowd surged around the massive stone walls. Soldiers joined them and brought cannons. Amid smoke and fire, the people stormed the gates of the fortress.

The Defarges were at the head of the crowd.

Once inside, the attackers spread across the courtyard, into every corner of the prison. They were going to seize the guards and force them to release the prisoners.

The poor people of Paris were full of fury. If they could, they would have torn apart the Bastille with their bare hands.

But Monsieur Defarge was on a different mission.

He grabbed a guard and said: 'One Hundred and Five, North Tower? It is a cell in this prison, yes?'

The terrified guard nodded.

'Show it to me! And bring a torch with you.'

Defarge and another man called Jacques followed the guard, who held a burning torch. He led them along stony passageways and up rugged stairs. The noise of the raging crowd grew distant.

After a while, the guard stopped at a low door. He put a key in the lock and swung the door open. As they all bent their heads to enter, he said: 'One Hundred and Five, North Tower!'

In the room was a stool, table and straw bed. There was a barred window high in the wall. There

was also an open hearth full
of wood ash. The chimney had
bars inside to prevent anybody
climbing in or out that way.

'Pass that torch slowly along
these walls,' said Defarge to the
guard.

The man obeyed. Defarge followed the smoky light closely with his eyes.

'Stop!' cried Defarge. 'Look here, Jacques!'

'A.M.!' read Jacques. 'Alexandre Manette.'

Defarge traced the letters scratched into the stone. Next to "A.M." were the words "A POOR DOCTOR".

'It's his cell, for sure,' said Defarge, more to himself than to Jacques or the guard.

He told the guard to hold the torch higher. Then he ducked into the hearth and peered up the chimney.

Defarge had brought a crowbar with him. He scraped at the iron grating inside the chimney. Flakes of soot and tiny pieces of stone pattered onto his head but he paid no attention.

The other two men couldn't see what he was doing, but Defarge

seemed to be reaching for something
that was hidden inside the chimney.
As he emerged, he tucked an item
into his dusty, sooty shirt.

'What's that?' said Jacques.

'Nothing,' said Defarge.

Of course, it was not nothing. What Monsieur Defarge had recovered from inside the chimney was a true story, written by Dr Manette in the dim light of his cell. It explained how he had come to be in prison, and who had put him there.

Long ago, Dr Manette had been summoned to attend to an injured

young man. He was taken to a grand house. It belonged to the Marquis St Evrémonde, a cruel man. This greedy man did as he pleased to the poor peasants who worked themselves to the bone for him.

The injured young man was not part of St Evrémonde's family. He was the brother of a beautiful peasant girl the Marquis had his eye on. When the girl's brother tried to stop the Marquis from taking her away, Evrémonde stabbed him. Dr Manette did everything he could for the dying brother, but he could not save him.

The doctor protested to the Marquis St Evrémonde. But the Marquis told Dr Manette that the young man's life mattered no more than the game birds he shot from the sky, or the deer he hunted for pleasure.

The Marquis tried to bribe Dr Manette. He offered him a huge pile of gold in exchange for his silence about the killing, but the doctor pushed the glittering coins back.

Dr Manette wrote a letter to the French government. He did not expect much to be done. Nobles like the Marquis were powerful and

protected. He realised just how much
when he was called to another urgent
medical case.

The Marquis and some other men
were in the coach that came to collect
him. The Marquis took the letter the
doctor had written and burnt it in his
lantern. The doctor was blindfolded,
and taken to the Bastille.

There he stayed for many years,

in a remote, secret cell: One Hundred and Five, North Tower.

Dr Manette had hoped that someday his written story would be discovered and that the Marquis would be punished for his crime. He ended his tale by cursing the Evrémonde family.

London

The storm of the French Revolution was heard and felt across the Channel, in London.

It was heard and felt by Charles Darnay.

Darnay was the name that Charles had given himself. He was ashamed of his real name. He was ashamed of the family into which he had been born: the St Evrémondes. The Marquis was his uncle, but Charles's father was just as bad.

Despairing of his family and their cruel ways, Charles had escaped to England. He changed his name and resolved to live simply and honestly, and to earn his own money.

He felt bound to tell Dr Manette his real name on the morning of his marriage to Lucie. That was why the doctor had been so shaken that the colour drained from his face. His beloved daughter's husband-to-be was the nephew of the man who had left him to rot away in the Bastille! But the doctor knew that Charles was a good man. He was completely different from the older members of his family.

There was no reason for Charles to ever return to France, especially now that his father and his uncle were dead. The grand house outside Paris had been burnt to the ground.

But the common people of France had risen up against their cruel rulers. They were not satisfied by a few great houses burning to the ground. Or by a handful of rich nobles being beheaded with the guillotine. They wanted more. They were full of rage and revenge. They didn't care if they destroyed the innocent along with the guilty.

There had been a steward called Gabelle on Charles's uncle's estate. Gabelle was a kind man, but because of his connection to the Evrémondes he was threatened with death.

He wrote to Charles for help. At great risk, Charles decided to return

to Paris and defend the steward. He did not tell Lucie or Dr Manette. He knew that they would prevent him from leaving. Instead, he wrote them each a letter, explaining his reasons. Then, one evening, he slipped away from the house in London and set off for Paris.

PARIS

Charles ran into trouble as soon as he arrived back in France. He was an aristocrat, one of the hated class of people, like his uncle and father. He was a St Evrémonde.

Charles was dragged to Paris and thrown into a prison called La Force. There, traitors and aristocrats were put on trial.

Often, they were sent to the guillotine to be beheaded.

Charles was in danger because of his family name. Gabelle the steward was released, but Charles was imprisoned in his place. Lucie and Dr Manette heard this frightening news and travelled to Paris. They were accompanied by Jarvis Lorry and Sydney Carton. Carton had been a student in Paris and knew the city well. The four of them were desperate to rescue Charles.

Dr Manette believed he may have some influence over the people. He had been a victim of the old system they were rebelling against. He had been

punished for helping the poor. Surely
Charles's accusers would listen to *him*?

For the second time in his life,
Charles was brought before a court.
He was faced by several judges
and prosecutors.

The crowd in the courtroom cried out for his head to be chopped off. They said that he was an enemy of the state. But Charles answered the judges' accusations calmly. He said he was the son-in-law of Alexandre Manette. The doctor then spoke on Charles's behalf. For a time, it

seemed as though all would be well and Charles would be saved. But there was a surprise witness. Two surprise witnesses, in fact.

Monsieur and Madame Defarge.

Madame Defarge sat at the back on the courtroom. She knitted as if her knitting needles were daggers. She watched her husband produce

the ragged sheets of paper he'd retrieved from the chimney of the doctor's prison cell.

Dr Manette's story was read out to the court. The death of the young man stabbed by the Marquis St Evrémonde was revealed.

Then Madame Defarge gave witness. She declared that she was the sister of the dead man. She demanded that the St Evrémonde family be destroyed, just as her family had been destroyed long ago.

Dr Manette, too, in his prison cell, had cursed the St Evrémondes. Without knowing it, he had signed a death warrant for his own son-in-law.

Worse still, the Defarges were so set on vengeance that they began to

plot against Lucie, too. After all, she

was a St Evrémonde by marriage.

Charles spent his last night in his
cell in La Force. Again, he wrote to
his wife and to his father-in-law. He
asked Dr Manette to care for Lucie
and their young daughter. He tried
to distract himself from what was to
come with visions of their life back
in London.

He heard a clock outside striking the hours. Nine … ten … eleven … It was the final time he would hear those hours.

There were footsteps in the stone passage outside the door.

The key turned in the lock.

The door quickly opened and closed. There before him stood Sydney Carton.

Sydney put his finger to his lips.' The guards are outside. I have bribed both of them.'

'What are you doing here?' said Charles.

'Hurry,' said Sydney. 'We have little time. Swap boots with me. Swap your scarf and coat for mine. Quick!'

'Sydney, there is no escaping from this place. You will die with me. It is madness.'

'It would be madness if I asked *you* to escape. But you are escaping as *me*.'

Charles was confused. 'But what are you going to do?'

'I shall stay here. Listen, Charles: Jarvis Lorry is waiting in a carriage outside. You'll be reunited with Lucie and Dr Manette. Using my name, you can all escape back to England.'

Charles was tempted for a moment. The promise of freedom! Of seeing his wife and daughter again!

Yet he said: 'I cannot allow you to do this. You are no more guilty than I am.'

'I have no wife or child,' said Sydney. 'And I have never valued my own life very much.'

86

When Charles was sentenced,
Sydney had decided to save him,
even if it meant dying in his place.
Just as he had helped Charles in the
Old Bailey by showing how similar
they looked,
Sydney would
act as Charles's
double now.

He knew that
Charles would
not escape

willingly, so Sydney cleverly
distracted him. Then he pressed
a handkerchief over his mouth

and nose. The handkerchief was soaked in a liquid that would make Charles suddenly fall asleep.

While Charles slept, Sydney quickly swapped clothes with him. Then he knocked on the cell door. When the guards entered, Sydney spoke and acted exactly like Charles.

'My friend has been overcome by distress at seeing me here,' he said. 'Take him to the main gate. A carriage is waiting.'

The guards carried Charles out, believing him to be Sydney Carton.

The plan worked. Charles was placed in the carriage with Jarvis Lorry, Lucie and her father. Every time they passed a checkpoint, they feared being discovered and arrested. But the red-capped soldiers and citizens accepted the identity papers naming the fourth occupant of the carriage as Sydney Carton, a lawyer from London.

When they reached the coast, they boarded a little boat to England. They were finally safe. But from that day on, they never forgot the name of their protector and saviour. When Lucie had another child, a boy, they named him Sydney in Sydney Carton's honour.

ဟ~

And what happened to Sydney Carton? A few hours after he had helped Charles escape his cell in La Force, he was taken to be killed.

The crowd gathered round the guillotine. They were impressed by how peaceful and calm Syndey seemed.

As reviewed his life in his last moments, Sydney had no regrets.

He thought: *It is a far, far better thing*

that I do, than I have ever done. It is a far, far better rest that I go to, than I have ever known.

Charles Dickens

Charles Dickens was born in Portsmouth in 1812. Like many of the characters he wrote about, his family were poor and his childhood was difficult. As an adult, he became known around the world for his books. He is remembered as one of the most important writers of his time.